The
HELEN OXENBURY
Nursery Story Book

The
HELEN OXENBURY
Nursery Story Book

HEINEMANN · LONDON

William Heinemann Ltd
10 Upper Grosvenor Street, London W1X 9PA

LONDON MELBOURNE TORONTO
JOHANNESBURG AUCKLAND

First published 1985
Text compilation and illustrations © Helen Oxenbury 1985
Reprinted 1986
434 95602 3

Printed in Italy

Contents

Goldilocks and the Three Bears

Once upon a time, there were three bears who lived together in their own little house in the wood. There was a great big father bear, a middle-sized mother bear and a little baby bear. They each had a special bowl for porridge, a special chair for sitting in, and a special bed to sleep in.

One morning the mother bear made their porridge for breakfast and poured it out into the great big bowl, the middle-sized bowl and the little baby bowl. But it was so hot the bears decided to go for a walk while it cooled.

Now a little girl called Goldilocks was walking in the woods that morning and she came across the bears' house. She knocked on the door and when there was no reply, she crept slowly in.

''Oh! Oh!'' she cried when she saw the bowls of porridge. ''I'm so hungry; I must have just one spoonful.''

First she went to the great big bowl and took a taste. ''Too hot!'' she said.

Then she went to the middle-sized bowl and tried that porridge. ''Too cold,'' she said.

Last she went to the little baby bowl. ''Oh! Oh! Just right!'' she cried, and she ate it all up, every bit.

Then Goldilocks saw the great big chair and climbed into it. ''Too big,'' she said, and climbed down quickly.

Next she went to the middle-sized chair and sat down. ''Too hard,'' she said.

Then she went quickly to the little baby chair. ''It just fits,'' she said happily. But really the chair was too small for her and – CRACK – it broke, and down she tumbled.

Then she went into the next room where she saw three neat beds. First she climbed into the great big bed, but it was too high. Next she climbed into the middle-sized bed, but it was too low.

Then she saw the little baby bed. "Oh! Oh!" she cried. "This is just right." She got in, pulled up the covers, and went fast asleep.

Before long the three bears came home for their breakfast. First the great big bear went to eat his porridge.

He took one look and said in his great rough voice, "Somebody has been eating my porridge!"

Then the middle-sized bear looked into her bowl and said in her middle-sized voice, "And somebody has been eating my porridge, too!"

Finally the little baby bear went to his bowl. "Oh! Oh!" he cried in his little baby voice. "Somebody's been eating my porridge and has eaten it all up!"

After that, all three bears wanted to sit down. The great big bear went to his great big chair and saw that the cushion had been squashed down. "Somebody has been sitting in my chair," he cried in his great big voice.

Then the middle-sized mother bear went to her middle-sized chair and found her cushion on the floor. "Somebody has been sitting in my chair," she said in her middle-sized voice.

Then the little baby bear hurried to his chair. "Oh! Oh!" he cried in his little baby voice "Somebody's been sitting in my chair and broken it all to bits!"

The three bears, feeling very sad, went into the bedroom.

First the great big bear looked at his bed. "Somebody has been lying in my bed," he said in his great big voice.

Then the middle-sized bear saw her bed all rumpled up and she cried in her middle-sized voice, "Oh dear, somebody has been lying in my bed."

By this time the little baby bear had gone to his little baby bed and he cried, "Somebody has been lying in my bed, and she's still here!"

This time his little baby voice was so high and squeaky that Goldilocks woke up with a start and sat up. There on one side of the bed were the three bears all looking down at her.

Now Goldilocks did not know that they were kind bears

and she was very frightened. She screamed, jumped out of bed, ran to the open window and quickly climbed out. Then she ran home to her mother as fast as she possibly could.

As for the bears, they put things to rights, and since Goldilocks never came again, they lived happily ever after.

The Turnip

Once there was a man who lived with his wife and little boy in a cottage in the country. One morning in May the man planted some turnip seeds.

Before long little turnip leaves began to poke up through the brown earth. Then an odd thing happened. One turnip plant began to grow faster than all the rest. It grew and it grew and it grew.

"We must have that turnip for supper tonight," said the man.

So he tried to pull the big turnip out of the ground. He pulled and he pulled and he pulled. But the turnip stuck fast.

"Wife, wife," he called, "come and help me pull this great turnip."

His wife came running. Then she pulled the man, and the man pulled the turnip. Oh how hard they pulled! But the turnip stuck fast.

''Son, son,'' called his mother, ''come and help us pull this big turnip out of the ground.''

The little boy came running and took tight hold of his mother. Then the boy pulled his mother, his mother pulled his father, and his father pulled the turnip. But still it stuck fast.

Then the little boy whistled for his dog.

''Come and help us,'' the boy said.

So the dog pulled the boy, the boy pulled his mother, his mother pulled his father and his father pulled the turnip. But still it stuck fast.

Then the dog barked for the hen.

The hen came flying and grabbed tight hold of the dog's tail. Then she pulled the dog, the dog pulled the boy, the boy pulled his mother, his mother pulled his father, and his father pulled the turnip. But still the turnip stuck fast.

''Cluck, cluck, cluck!'' cried the hen.

And the cock came flying to help. Then the cock pulled the hen, the hen pulled the dog, the dog pulled the boy, the boy pulled his mother, his mother pulled his father, his father pulled the turnip and . . .

(15)

Whoosh! . . . Up came the turnip out of the ground, and down, backwards, they all tumbled in a heap. But they weren't hurt a bit and just got up laughing.

Then they rolled the turnip into the house and the boy's mother cooked it for their supper. Everyone had all they could eat and still there was enough left over for the next day, and the next, and the day after that!

The Little Porridge Pot

There was once a little girl who lived in a village with her mother. They were very poor and things got worse and worse until one day they found that there was nothing left to eat.

"I'll go into the forest and see if I can find some berries," the little girl said. And off she went.

She had not gone far when she met a very old woman who smiled at her. "I know that you are a good little girl and that you and your mother are poor and hungry. Here is a little pot to take home. Whenever you say to it, 'Cook, little pot,' it will fill itself full of delicious steaming porridge. When you have had all you can eat, you must say, 'Enough, little pot,' and it will stop making porridge."

The little girl thanked the kind old woman and took the pot home to her mother. They were both so hungry that they could scarcely wait to say, "Cook, little pot."

At once the pot was full of porridge. Then, when they had eaten all they could, the little girl said, "Enough, little pot," and it was empty again.

From that day on, the little girl and her mother were never hungry anymore, and they lived very happily for a while.

But one day when the little girl was out her mother wanted some of that delicious porridge all for herself. Carefully, she got the pot down from the shelf and said the magic words, "Cook, little pot." In a moment the pot was full.

The little girl's mother ate as much as she wanted. Then, suddenly, she screamed.

"Oh dear! Oh dear! I can't remember how to make it stop!"

The porridge kept on coming and coming. It filled the little pot to the brim. It seeped over the top and down onto the table. Bubbling and steaming, it overflowed onto the floor. More and more kept coming. The porridge ran across the floor and out of the door and streamed down the street. It went into neighbours' gardens! And into

their houses! Finally, there was only one house in the whole village that wasn't filled with porridge!

"Oh! Oh! Oh!" all the villagers cried at once. "Whatever shall we do?"

At that very moment, the little girl came home, and seeing porridge everywhere, she cried, "Enough, little pot."

To everyone's relief, the porridge stopped coming. However, they all had to squeeze into the one house that had escaped and live there together until, at last, they could eat their way back to their own homes.

The Three Little Pigs

Once there were three little pigs who grew up and left their mother to find homes for themselves.

The first little pig set out, and before long he met a man with a bundle of straw.

"Please, Man," said the pig, "will you let me have that bundle of straw to build my house?"

"Yes, here, take it," said the kind man.

The little pig was very pleased and at once built himself a house of straw.

He had hardly moved in when a wolf came walking by, and, seeing the new house, knocked on the door.

"Little pig, little pig," he said, "open up the door and let me in."

Now the little pig's mother had warned him about strangers, so he said, "No, not by the hair of my chinny-chin-chin, I'll not let you in."

"Then I'll huff and I'll puff and I'll blow your house down!" cried the wolf.

But the little pig went on saying, "No, not by the hair of my chinny-chin-chin, I'll not let you in."

So the old wolf huffed and he puffed and he blew the house down, and ate up the little pig.

The second little pig said good-bye to his mother and set out. Before long he met a man with a bundle of sticks.

"Please, Man," he said, "will you let me have that bundle of sticks to build my house?"

"Yes, you can have it. Here it is," said the kind man.

So the second little pig was very pleased and used the sticks to build himself a house. He had hardly moved in when the wolf came walking by and knocked at the door.

"Little pig, little pig," he said, "open up your door and let me in."

Now the second little pig remembered what his mother had told him, so he, too, said, "No, not by the hair of my chinny-chin-chin, I'll not let you in."

"Then I'll huff and I'll puff and I'll blow your house down!" cried the wolf.

But the little pig went on saying, "No, not by the hair of my chinny-chin-chin, I'll not let you in!"

So again, the old wolf huffed and he puffed, and he

huffed and he puffed. This time it was much harder work but, finally, down came the house and he ate up the second little pig.

Then, last of all, the third little pig set out and met a man with a load of bricks.

"Please, Man," he said, "will you let me have that load of bricks to build my house?"

"Yes, here they are – all for you," said the kind man.

The third little pig was very pleased, and built himself a brick house.

Again the wolf came along, and again he said, "Little pig, little pig, open your door and let me in."

But, like his brothers, the third little pig said, "No, not by the hair of my chinny-chin-chin, I'll not let you in."

"Then I'll huff and I'll puff and I'll blow your house down!" cried the wolf.

And when the third little pig wouldn't open the door, he huffed and he puffed, and he huffed and he puffed. Then he tried again but the brick house was so strong that he could not blow it down.

This made the wolf so angry that he jumped onto the roof of the little brick house and roared down the chimney, "I'm coming down to eat you up!"

The little pig had put a pot full of boiling water on the fire and now he took off the lid. Down the chimney tumbled the wolf and – SPLASH – he fell right into the pot.

Quickly, the little pig banged on the cover and boiled up the old wolf for his dinner.

And so the clever little pig lived happily ever after.

The Gingerbread Boy

There was once a woman who hadn't any children of her own and wanted one very much. One day she said to her husband, "I shall bake myself a nice gingerbread boy. That's what I shall do."

Her husband laughed at this idea but that very morning she mixed the dough and rolled it. Then she cut out a little boy shape with a smiling mouth and two currants for eyes. When she had popped him in the oven, she waited for him to bake and then she opened the door. Out jumped the gingerbread boy and ran away through the kitchen and right outside.

"Husband, husband," called the woman as she ran after the gingerbread boy.

The man dropped his spade when he heard his wife call and came running from the field.

But when the gingerbread boy saw the woman and the man chasing him, he only laughed, running faster and faster and shouting:

> *"Run, run, as fast as you can,*
> *You can't catch me,*
> *I'm the gingerbread man!"*

On he ran until he met a cow.

"Moo! Moo!" called the cow. "Stop! Stop! I want to eat you."

But the gingerbread boy only laughed and ran faster than ever, shouting, "I've run away from a woman and a man and now I'll run away from you!

(33)

"Run, run, as fast as you can,
You can't catch me,
I'm the gingerbread man!"

The cow chased after him but she was too fat and couldn't catch him. He raced on until he came to a horse.

"Neigh! Neigh!" snorted the horse. "You look good to eat. Stop and let me gobble you up."

But the gingerbread boy only laughed and shouted, "I've run away from a woman, a man, and a cow, and now I'll run away from you!

"Run, run, as fast as you can,
You can't catch me,
I'm the gingerbread man!"

The horse galloped after the gingerbread boy but couldn't catch him. He raced on faster and faster until he came to some farmers in a field.

"Ho! Ho!" they cried. "Stop! Stop! and let us have a bite."

But the gingerbread boy only laughed and shouted, "I've run away from a woman, a man, a cow, a horse, and now I'll run away from you!

"Run, run, as fast as you can,
You can't catch me,
I'm the gingerbread man!"

The men joined in the chase but no one could catch the
gingerbread boy. He raced far ahead until he came to a

river and had to stop. There he met a fox who wanted very much to eat him then and there, but he was afraid the clever gingerbread boy might escape.

So he said politely, "Do you want to cross the river?"

"Yes, please," said the gingerbread boy.

"Well, then, jump on my back and I'll swim across."

"Thank you," said the gingerbread boy; and he did just that.

When they were about halfway across, the fox said, "The water is deeper here. I think you'd better crawl up onto my neck."

"Thank you," said the gingerbread boy; and he did just that.

When they had gone three-quarters of the way across,

the fox said, "You'd better climb up onto my head. You can't be very comfortable there."

"Thank you," said the gingerbread boy; and he did just that.

"We're nearly there now," said the fox a moment later. "I think you'll be safer if you get onto my nice long nose."

"Thank you," said the gingerbread boy. But no sooner had he climbed onto the fox's nose than the fox threw back his head and SNAP! went his big mouth.

The gingerbread boy was half gone.

Then the fox did it again, SNAP!

The gingerbread boy was three-quarters gone.

The fox was having a very good time, and he did it again. SNAP!

The gingerbread boy was all gone.

And that was the end of the gingerbread boy who had been too clever for the woman, the man, the cow, the horse, and the farmers. But not clever enough for the fox.

Henny-Penny

One day when Henny-Penny was scratching about for corn in the farmyard, an acorn fell down from the oak tree and hit her on the head.

"Goodness gracious," she cried, "the sky is falling. I must go and tell the king."

So, off she went in a great hurry and soon she met Cocky-Locky.

"Where are you going?" asked Cocky-Locky.

"I'm going to tell the king the sky is falling," said Henny-Penny.

"Can I come, too?" asked Cocky-Locky.

"Yes, do," said Henny-Penny.

So off went Henny-Penny and Cocky-Locky to tell the king the sky was falling, and, before long, they met Ducky-Daddles.

"Where are you going?" asked Ducky-Daddles.

"Oh, we're going to tell the king the sky is falling," said Henny-Penny and Cocky-Locky.

"Can I come, too?" asked Ducky-Daddles.

"Yes, do," said Henny-Penny and Cocky-Locky.

So off went Henny-Penny, Cocky-Locky and Ducky-Daddles to tell the king the sky was falling and, before long, they met Goosey-Poosey.

"Where are you going?" asked Goosey-Poosey.

"Oh, we're going to tell the king the sky is falling," said Henny-Penny, Cocky-Locky and Ducky-Daddles.

"Can I come, too?" asked Goosey-Poosey.

"Yes, do," said Henny-Penny, Cocky-Locky and Ducky-Daddles.

So off went Henny-Penny, Cocky-Locky, Ducky-Daddles and Goosey-Poosey to tell the king the sky was falling and, before long, they met Turkey-Lurkey.

"Where are you going?" asked Turkey-Lurkey.

"Oh, we're going to tell the king the sky is falling," said Henny-Penny, Cocky-Locky, Ducky-Daddles and Goosey-Poosey.

"Can I come, too?" asked Turkey-Lurkey.

"Yes, do," said Henny-Penny, Cocky-Locky, Ducky-Daddles and Goosey-Poosey.

So off went Henny-Penny, Cocky-Locky, Ducky-Daddles, Goosey-Poosey and Turkey-Lurkey to tell the king the sky was falling.

They went along together, Henny-Penny, Cocky-Locky, Ducky-Daddles, Goosey-Poosey and Turkey-Lurkey – along and along, until they met Foxy-Woxy.

"Where are you going?" asked Foxy-Woxy.

"Oh, we're going to tell the king the sky is falling," said Henny-Penny, Cocky-Locky, Ducky-Daddles, Goosey-Poosey and Turkey-Lurkey.

"But you're not going the right way," said Foxy-Woxy. "I know the right way. Let me show you."

"Thank you," said Henny-Penny, Cocky-Locky, Ducky-Daddles, Goosey-Poosey and Turkey-Lurkey.

So off they all went with Foxy-Woxy leading the way, and, before long, they came to a dark hole. Now this was really the home of Foxy-Woxy but he said, "This is the shortest way to the king's palace. Follow me."

So Foxy-Woxy went a little way down the hole and waited for Henny-Penny, Cocky-Locky, Ducky-Daddles, Goosey-Poosey and Turkey-Lurkey.

First came Turkey-Lurkey.

"Snap!" Foxy-Woxy bit off Turkey-Lurkey's head.

Next came Goosey-Poosey.

"Snap!" Foxy-Woxy bit off Goosey-Poosey's head.

Next came Ducky-Daddles.

"Snap!" Foxy-Woxy bit off Ducky-Daddles's head.

Next came Cocky-Locky.

"Snap!" But this time Foxy-Woxy was getting tired and he missed, so that Cocky-Locky managed to call out to Henny-Penny, "Look out! Don't come!"

Henny-Penny heard Cocky-Locky and ran back home to the farmyard as fast as she could go. And that was why she never told the king the sky was falling.

The Elves and the Shoemaker

Once there was a shoemaker who lived with his wife in a little cottage. They were poor and he found it hard to earn enough money to live on.

Finally the day came when they had no money and only a crust of bread for supper. However, there was just enough leather left to make one pair of shoes. The shoemaker cut out the pieces carefully and put them on his workbench ready to sew together in the morning.

He woke early next day and went to his bench to make his last pair of shoes. But instead of the pieces of leather he had left the night before, he found a finished pair of shoes. They were more beautiful than any the shoemaker had ever made.

"Wife, wife!" he called excitedly. "Come and tell me if I'm dreaming!"

At this his wife came running and when she looked, she cried, "Oh, no, you aren't dreaming. The shoes are finished and . . . and . . . oh, so beautiful, too!"

While the shoemaker and his wife were turning the shoes around in their hands to see the fine stitches, a grand gentleman came in. He saw the lovely new shoes and wanted to buy them then and there. What is more, he paid the shoemaker so much for them that the shoemaker was able to buy leather for two more pairs. He also bought some fresh bread, cheese and other good food.

In the afternoon he cut out the new leather carefully and put the pieces on his workbench ready to sew together in the morning. Then he and his wife sat down

together for the best meal they had had for a long time.
They went to bed very happy and slept soundly.

When they woke up next day, lo and behold, there
were two new pairs of shoes, all sewn and shining on the

workbench. That same day the grand gentleman came to buy shoes for all his family and took both of the new pairs. The shoemaker was able to buy enough leather for four more pairs, and there was money left over, too.

Again on the third night the same thing happened and in the morning they woke up to find four new pairs of lovely shoes. Then more friends of the grand gentleman came and every pair was gone in a twinkling. This went on from day to day until the shoemaker and his wife were growing rich.

One morning the shoemaker's wife said, ''We must try to find out who is being so kind so we can thank him.''

''I know what we'll do,'' said the shoemaker. ''Tonight we'll stay up and watch to see what happens.''

So that night they hid themselves in a corner of the room and waited.

At midnight they heard the front door open and then they saw two little naked elves come dancing in. The elves sat down at once and began to sew so fast that, in only a few moments, there was a whole row of perfect new shoes and every single piece of leather had been used. Then the elves climbed down from the bench and ran out the door.

Next morning the shoemaker's wife said, ''Now that we know who is helping us perhaps we can thank them in some way. I think they look cold without any clothes, poor things. I'm going to make them each a jacket and trousers and knit them some warm socks. It is getting colder every day and when the winter comes they will be frozen.''

''What a good idea,'' said her husband, ''and I will make them each a special pair of shoes.''

(51)

They both set to work that very day but it took them some time because they had to stay awake many nights and watch to make sure of the right size. At last it was Christmas Eve and the clothes and the shoes were finished. The shoemaker and his wife laid them out carefully on the bench instead of the usual pieces of leather. Then they stayed awake and listened for their little friends to come.

When the clock struck twelve slow strokes, the elves came dancing in. At first when they climbed on the bench they couldn't understand what had happened. Then one of them held up a little jacket and they both cried out, "Oh, look! Look! These are clothes to wear and they will just fit us!"

It took only a moment to put everything on, and last of all, they found two little pointed caps. Everything fitted so perfectly that the two little elves danced and sang with delight.

Then out of the door they ran, and after that Christmas Eve, they never came again. But all now went well for the shoemaker and his wife. They were never poor again but lived happily ever after.

The Three Billy Goats Gruff

Once upon a time there were three Billy Goats. Their names were Big Billy Goat Gruff, Little Billy Goat Gruff and Baby Billy Goat Gruff.

They had lived all winter on a rocky hillside where no grass or flowers grew for them to eat. By the time spring came and the weather began to get warmer, they were thin and very hungry.

But over the bridge on the other side of the river the hillside wasn't rocky at all. There the grass was thick and green with delicious flowers growing in it.

"We must cross the bridge to the other side where we can find plenty to eat," said Big Billy Goat Gruff.

"But the wicked Troll who lives under the bridge won't let anyone cross," said Baby Billy Goat Gruff.

The Billy Goats Gruff were afraid to cross the bridge but it was the only way to reach the lovely grass. They grew hungrier and hungrier every day until one day they put their heads together and made a plan.

First Baby Billy Goat Gruff went down the hillside and started across the bridge.

"Who goes there?" cried the Troll.

"It's only me, Baby Billy Goat Gruff."

"I'll eat you up," screamed the Troll. "I eat anyone who dares to cross my bridge."

"But I'm so small I'm only a mouthful," said the littlest Billy Goat Gruff. "If you wait for my bigger brother, he'll be along in a few minutes."

"Oh, all right," said the Troll crossly.

So Baby Billy Goat Gruff went safely over the bridge.

(55)

Before long the next brother, Little Billy Goat Gruff, came to the bridge.

At once the Troll roared, ''You can't cross my bridge. I'm going to eat you up!''

Little Billy Goat Gruff leaned over the side and called down to him, ''I'm only a bit bigger than my baby brother and scarcely more than two mouthfuls. Wait for my big brother who will be coming along soon.''

''Oh, very well then,'' said the Troll, ''but I'm getting very hungry and I won't wait much longer.''

Before the old Troll could change his mind, Little Billy Goat Gruff was across the bridge and away up the hill to join his brother.

It wasn't long before Big Billy Goat Gruff came down the hill and started to cross the bridge. At once the Troll jumped out from underneath and reached up to catch him. But Big Billy Goat Gruff was very strong and he butted the Troll hard with his great horns. He tossed him high in the air and then . . . splash ! . . . down . . . down he went, right into the middle of the river.

How Big Billy Goat laughed as he dashed across the bridge and up the hillside to join his two brothers.

Little Red Riding Hood

There was once a little girl whose mother made her a new cloak with a hood. It was a lovely red colour and she liked to wear it so much that everyone called her Little Red Riding Hood.

One day her mother said to her, "I want you to take this basket of cakes to your grandmother who is ill."

Little Red Riding Hood liked to walk through the woods to her grandmother's cottage and she quickly put on her cloak. As she was leaving, her mother said, "Now remember, don't talk to any strangers on the way."

But Little Red Riding Hood loved talking to people, and as she was walking along the path, she met a wolf.

"Good morning, Little Girl, where are you off to in your beautiful red cloak?" said the wolf with a wicked smile.

Little Red Riding Hood put down her basket and said, "I'm taking some cakes to my grandmother who's not very well."

"Where does your grandmother live?" asked the wolf.

"In the cottage at the end of this path," said Little Red Riding Hood.

Now the wolf was really very hungry and he wanted to eat up Little Red Riding Hood then and there. But he heard a woodcutter not far away and he ran off.

He went straight to the grandmother's cottage where he found the old woman sitting up in bed. Before she knew what was happening, he ate her up in one gulp. Then he put on the grandmother's nightdress and her nightcap, and climbed into her bed. He snuggled well

down under the bedclothes and tried to hide himself.

Before long, Little Red Riding Hood came to the door with her basket of cakes and knocked.

''Come in,'' said the wolf, trying to make his voice sound soft.

At first, when she went in, Little Red Riding Hood thought that her grandmother must have a bad cold.

She went over to the bed. ''What big eyes you have, Grandmama,'' she said, as the wolf peered at her from under the nightcap.

''All the better to see you with, my dear,'' said the wolf.

''What big ears you have, Grandmama.''

''All the better to hear you with, my dear,'' answered the wolf.

Then Little Red Riding Hood saw a long nose and a wide-open mouth. She wanted to scream but she said, very bravely, ''What a big mouth you have, Grandmama.''

At this the wolf opened his jaws wide. ''All the better to eat you with!'' he cried. And he jumped out of bed and ate up Little Red Riding Hood.

Just at that moment the woodcutter passed by the

cottage. Noticing that the door was open, he went inside. When he saw the wolf he quickly swung his axe and chopped off his head.

Little Red Riding Hood and then her grandmother stepped out, none the worse for their adventure.

Little Red Riding Hood thanked the woodcutter and ran home to tell her mother all that had happened. And after that day, she never, ever, spoke to strangers.

The Little Red Hen

Once there was a pretty, neat little house. Inside it lived a Cock, a Mouse and a Little Red Hen.

On another hill, not far away, was a very different little house. It had a door that wouldn't shut, windows that were dirty and broken, and the paint was peeling off. In this house lived a bad old mother Fox and her fierce young son.

One morning the mother Fox said, "On the hill over there you can see the house where the Cock, the Mouse and the Little Red Hen live. You and I haven't had very much to eat for a long time, and everyone in that house is very well fed and plump. They would make us a delicious dinner!"

The fierce young Fox was very hungry, so he got up at once and said, "I'll just find a sack. If you will get the big pot boiling, I'll go to that house on the hill and we'll have that Cock, that Mouse and that Little Red Hen for our dinner!"

Now on the very same morning the Little Red Hen got up early, as she always did, and went downstairs to get the breakfast. The Cock and the Mouse, who were lazy, did not come downstairs for some time.

"Who will get some sticks to light the fire?" asked the Little Red Hen.

"I won't," said the Cock.

"I won't," said the Mouse.

"Then I'll have to do it myself," said the Little Red Hen. So off she ran to get the sticks.

When she had the fire burning, she said, "Who will go

and get the kettle filled with water from the spring?"

"I won't," said the Cock again.

"I won't," said the Mouse again.

"Then I'll have to do it myself," said the Little Red Hen, and off she ran to fill the kettle.

While they were waiting for their breakfast, the Cock and the Mouse curled up in comfortable armchairs. Soon they were asleep again.

It was just at this time that the fierce young Fox came up the hill with his sack and peeped in at the window. He stepped back and knocked loudly at the door.

"Who can that be?" said the Mouse, half opening his eyes.

"Go and find out, if you want to know," said the Cock crossly.

"Perhaps it's the postman," said the Mouse to himself. So, without waiting to ask who it was, he lifted the latch and opened the door.

In rushed the big fierce Fox!

"Cock-a-doodle-do!" screamed the Cock as he jumped onto the back of the armchair.

"Oh! Oh! Oh!" squeaked the Mouse as he tried to run up the chimney.

But the Fox only laughed. He grabbed the Mouse by the tail and popped him into the sack. Then he caught the Cock and pushed him in the sack too.

Just at that moment, in came the Little Red Hen, carrying the heavy kettle of water from the spring. Before she knew what was happening, the Fox quickly snatched her up and put her into the sack with the others. Then he tied a string tightly around the opening. And, with the sack over his shoulder, he set off down the hill.

The Cock, the Mouse and the Little Red Hen were bumped together uncomfortably inside the sack.

The Cock said, "Oh, I wish I hadn't been so cross!"

And the Mouse said, "Oh, I wish I hadn't been so lazy!"

But the Little Red Hen said, "It's never too late to try again."

As the Fox trudged along with his heavy load, the sun grew very hot. Soon, he put the sack on the ground and sat down to rest. Before long he was fast asleep. Then, "Gr——umph . . . gr——mph," he began to snore. The noise was so loud that the Little Red Hen could hear him through the sack.

At once she took her scissors out of her apron pocket and cut a neat hole in the sack. Then out jumped: first the Mouse, then the Cock, and last, the Little Red Hen.

"Quick! Quick!" she whispered. "Who will come and help me get some stones?"

"I will," said the Cock.

"And I will," said the Mouse.

"Good," said the Little Red Hen.

Off they went together and each one brought back as big a rock as he could carry and put it into the sack. Then the Little Red Hen, who had a needle and thread in her pocket too, sewed up the hole very neatly.

When she had finished, the Little Red Hen, the Cock and the Mouse ran off home as fast as they could go. Once inside, they bolted the door and then helped each other to get the best breakfast they had ever had!

After some time, the Fox woke up. He lifted the sack onto his back and went slowly up the hill to his house.

He called out, "Mother! Guess what I've got in my sack!"

"Is it – can it be – the Little Red Hen?"

"It is – and the Cock – and the Mouse as well. They're very plump and heavy so they'll make us a splendid dinner."

His mother had the water all ready, boiling furiously in a pot over the fire. The Fox undid the string and emptied the sack straight into the pot.

Splash! Splash! Splash! In went the three heavy rocks and out came the boiling hot water, all over the fierce young Fox and his bad old mother. Oh, how sore and burned and angry they were!

Never again did those wicked foxes trouble the Cock, the Mouse and the Little Red Hen, who always kept their door locked, and lived happily ever after.